D0548882

Chaconas, Dori

HACONAS,
ORI   Virginnie's Hat

$16.99

DATE DUE

MAY 2 0 2007		
JUL 0 6 2007		
OCT 0 9 2014		

DEMCO 128-5046

For Stacy and Kelly, with much love
D. C.

Text copyright © 2007 by Dori Chaconas
Illustrations copyright © 2007 by Holly Meade

Ingram 5-1-07 $16.99 / 9.43

All rights reserved. No part of this book may be reproduced, transmitted, or stored in an information retrieval
system in any form or by any means, graphic, electronic, or mechanical, including photocopying, taping, and
recording, without prior written permission from the publisher.

First edition 2007

Library of Congress Cataloging-in-Publication Data
Chaconas, Dori, date.
Virginnie's hat / Dori Chaconas ; illustrated by Holly Meade. —1st ed.
p. cm.
Summary: Determined to retrieve her hat from the sycamore tree where it had
been blown by the wind, Virginnie tries to dislodge it by throwing her boots up one by one,
unaware of the threatening swamp creatures behind her.
ISBN: 978-0-7636-2397-5
[1. Hats—Fiction. 2. Swamps—Fiction. 3. Stories in rhyme.] I. Meade, Holly, ill. II. Title
PZ8.3.C345Vir 2007
[E]—dc22   2006051856

2 4 6 8 10 9 7 5 3 1

Printed in Singapore

This book was typeset in Journal.
The illustrations were done in watercolor and collage.

Candlewick Press
2067 Massachusetts Avenue
Cambridge, Massachusetts 02140

visit us at www.candlewick.com

VIRGINNIE'S HAT

Dori Chaconas

illustrated by Holly Meade

CANDLEWICK PRESS
CAMBRIDGE, MASSACHUSETTS

Saguache County Public Library
Saguache, Colorado

Virginnie is a freckly gal.
That southern sun will toast her nose!
She buys a pretty wide-brimmed hat
To shade her clear down to her toes.

But . . .

A puff,
  a pull,

A whift,
  a lift,

A gust of wind—

that hat's adrift!

Right to the swamp
Just sailin' free,
Then that new hat
Lands high, high, high . . .
In a sycamore tree.

The swamp is dark
With oaks 'n' pines,
All twisty through
With kudzu vines.

The tree, so tall!
That hat won't budge.
"If I could give it
Just one nudge . . ."

High above Virginnie's head,

That pretty hat is stuck, all right.

She bends right down and grabs her boot,

Then throws it high with all her might.

Meanwhile . . .

Crawdaddy craw
Crawdaddy craw
Inching along
With a snap of his claw.

Close to the ground
Ugly and lean
Wanting to *pinch*—
Just to be mean—

Those toes!

But then . . .
Down!
falls the boot.

"Ack?" croaks the craw.

SPLACK!
smacks the boot
On the craw's sharp claw.
Shakin' with shock,
He scoots under a rock.

Virginnie grabs her other boot.
She throws it high into the air.
It spins and flies right toward the hat!
A tad too short! The hat stays there.

Meanwhile . . .

Snickery snake
Snickery snake
Slickers along
With a hunger-ly ache.

Looking for lunch
To ease his woes.
Seeing some lunch—
Little girl toes!

Some yum!

But then . . .

Down!

drops the boot.

Down!
Down!

SPLACK!

The boot lands smack on

The snake's long back.

So he slunkers away

For less dangerous prey.

Virginnie throws each boot again,
Then both together, left and right.
They whiz right up there through the air
In one knee-slappin', *yee-haw* flight.

Meanwhile . . .

Sway, gator, sway,
Comin' this way,
Cursed with a hunger
That's ruinin' his day.

Looking to munch on
Something sooo sweet,
Looking to lunch on—
Little girl feet!

Sweet!

Feet!

But . . .

Virginnie? Well, she's turned away.
She doesn't see that gator there.
She only sees that tumblin' boot
Knock that hat clear into the air!

Down! floats the hat,
Floot! Fleet! Flit!
She jumps! She grabs!
She catches it!

Virginnie's shriek is mighty loud!
It stabs right through that gator's head.
He flips around and hightails home
To put his aching ears to bed.

And then . . .

Virginnie hears a squishy step!

Her heart's a-floppin' with a scare.

She sees the grasses quickly part . . .

And look! It's Mama standing there!

"Mama! Don't you scare me so!
I thought you were a big ol' bear!"

"I heard you holler," Mama said.

"Why, sakes! What are you doing there?

Don't you know this swamp's alive

With critters that'll chomp and chew?"

"But, Ma! I didn't see a thing!
The only scary thing was you!"